This book may be kept

# SEVEN DAYS

A fine will be charged for each day the book is kept overtime.

10540

JE

Kent, Jack, 1920-
    The wizard of Wallaby Wallow.    N.Y.,
Parents magazine press, c1971.
    unp.    col.illus.

## EAU CLAIRE DISTRICT LIBRARY

I.Title.

RBP

# The WIZARD of Wallaby Wallow

by JACK KENT

*Parents' Magazine Press / New York*

*To Tony*

The Wizard of Wallaby Wallow
was very busy. He was trying to get
his stock of magic spells in order.

He had spells for turning folks into
everything from an aardvark to a zebu.
Each spell was in a little bottle
with a label on it which told what
sort of spell it was. But everything
was in such a jumble that it took the
wizard hours to find the one he wanted.
So he had cleared all the shelves
and was very carefully putting the
spells back in alphabetical order.

The spells for turning folks into angleworms, ants, and antelopes went on the shelf marked "A." Bears, bees, and buffaloes went on the "B" shelf. And so on.

"I wonder what sort of spell *this* is," said the wizard, studying the bottle he had just picked up. "The label has come off."

Just then there was a knock on the door.
"Oh, geese fleece!" swore the wizard.
"I'm never left·alone long enough to get
anything done."

He opened the door and said, "Go away.
I'm busy. Shoo!"

But the visitor was a mouse and quite used
to having folks yell *shoo* at him, so he
didn't pay any attention to the wizard.

"I want to buy a magic spell," the mouse said.

"I'm tired of being a mouse. Nobody likes
mice. They set traps for us and sic cats
on us and yell *shoo* at us and chase us with
brooms. It's not a very pleasant life. I
want to be something else."

"Like what?" asked the wizard.

"I haven't made up my mind," said the mouse. "I thought I'd come and see what sort of spells you had and choose one."

"Everything's in a mess
right now," said the wizard.
"Come back tomorrow and…

"wait a minute!" he said, remembering
the bottle in his hand.

"Here. You can have this one. No charge."
And he handed the bottle to the mouse.

"There isn't any label on it," said
the mouse. "What will it turn me into?"

"Something else," said the wizard.

"That's what you said you wanted to be!"
And he slammed the door
and went back to sorting his spells.

The mouse went home and set the bottle
in the middle of the dining-room table.
While he was looking for something to
pull the cork out with, he tried to guess
what the magic spell would turn him into.

A butterfly, perhaps?
Butterflies are pretty, but
they don't live very long.
He'd rather not be a butterfly.

Turtles live a long time, but they aren't very pretty. And they're so slow. The mouse hoped he wouldn't turn into a turtle.

Bees are fast. But they work awfully hard. Work was not one of the mouse's favorite activities.

Ants go on picnics.

But ants get stepped on.

Birds sing happy songs. But birds
eat worms. The thought made the mouse
a little ill.

"What if I turned into a *cat!*" the
mouse thought. "Cats eat mice!"
He turned pale at the thought.

"Or what if it's a spell for turning folks into mice? On me it wouldn't even show...

"like dribbling egg on a yellow bib.

"Now, if I turned into an elephant,
that would be worthwhile," thought
the mouse.

"But an elephant wouldn't fit in my house."
It was a nice little house. The mouse loved it very much. He hoped he wouldn't turn into an elephant.

In fact, he couldn't think of anything
the spell might turn him into that he
was sure he would enjoy being.
"Being me has its problems," he decided,
"but at least I know what they are.
Whatever I turn into might have bigger ones."

So he took the magic spell back to the wizard.

The wizard came mumbling and grumbling
to the door. He was still out of sorts
from sorting.

He didn't recognize the mouse at first.

"You've changed," the wizard said.
"I suppose I have," said the mouse.

"I was a very unhappy mouse before.
And now I'm...well...something
else."

"Was it the magic spell that changed you?"
asked the wizard.
"As a matter of fact, it was," said the mouse.

The wizard was so excited he could hardly speak.

"That's the first time one of my spells ever worked!" he said delightedly.

"Looks like it worked twice," said the mouse. "It made us *both* happy. It's a wonderful magic spell!"

The wizard went into his shop and took
the labels off all the bottles and raised the prices.

Then he put them back on the shelves
just any which way.

Sorting them was no longer a problem.

After that, whenever anyone in Wallaby Wallow felt unhappy with his lot, he knew what to do. He would buy one of the wizard's wonderful magic spells. They never failed to work—as long as the bottles weren't uncorked.